Cat and Mouse and the dinosaurs

Ray Gibson

Reading consultant: Karen Bryant-Mole

Illustrated by Graham Round

Designed by Amanda Barlow

Edited by Paula Borton

Parent's notes

This book is for you and your child to use together. It is aimed at children aged three and up who are just ready to learn to read their first words. It contains early reading activities which will help bridge the gap between prereading activities and first solo storybooks.

The main purpose of the book is to build your child's confidence and give a positive attitude for reading. It does not follow one particular method of teaching reading, but takes a varied approach which will not conflict with anything your child is learning at school.

On some pages there is just a simple story for you to read to your child. Being read to is a very important part of the process of learning to read. Feeling that books are a source of pleasure provides children with a strong incentive to read by themselves. It also helps to improve their listening and concentration skills and to develop their sense of what a story is.

There are instructions on each page to tell you what to do and footnotes to explain how the activity is contributing to your child's reading skills. The words in blue are for your child to read. Point them out and help your child to guess what they say.

The book builds towards a simple story for your child to read alone. The words used in the story are all introduced and used earlier in the book.

When tackling any of the activities in this book go at your child's natural pace and give plenty of praise and encouragement. It is very important that your reading sessions are enjoyable.

How do you know if your child is ready to read?

There is no definite way of knowing the answer to this. There are, however, some questions you could ask yourself to help you decide.

- Does your child like books?
- Does your child sometimes look at them alone?
- Does your child sometimes pretend she is reading?
- Does your child show an interest when you point out words, or write things down?
- Can your child recognize her own name?

- Does your child know a few letter sounds?
- Does your child ask you what words say?
- Does your child sometimes join in when you read stories she knows well?
- Can your child retell a simple story in the right sequence?

If your answer to most of these questions is "yes", then your child is probably ready to read.

Meet Cat and Mouse

This is Cat

This is Mouse

They live together in this house.

Whose chair is this?

Whose chair is that?

Who's reading? Is it Mouse or Cat?

They wish the rain would go away.

What can they find to do today?

Research has shown that recognizing and enjoying rhythm and rhyme helps children with the process of learning to read.

3

Something to do

Cat is feeling grumpy. He wants to play in the park, but it is still raining.

Mouse is busy reading and is taking no notice of Cat.

What can Cat do?

Suddenly, Mouse jumps up and points to the newspaper.
   "Look, we can go and see the dinosaurs at the museum, today."

Cat thinks this is a scary idea.
   "Dinosaurs!" Cat squeaks. "They're big and fierce with terrible teeth. They roar and bite, and lash their tails."

Come and see the dinosaurs at the museum.

Reading aloud to children helps to expand their vocabulary and concentration.

"These ones can't bite you, Cat," says Mouse. "They're only models someone has made. Real dinosaurs lived long ago."

"I knew that all the time," says Cat. "Will there be other things to see?"

"Dinosaur eggs in dinosaur nests, and dinosaur skeletons as big as a house," shouts Mouse, who is getting very excited.

Before they set off, Mouse shows Cat a book of dinosaurs and makes a list of the things they might see. See if you can match the words on the pictures with words on Mouse's list.

A big dinosaur

egg

nest

head

leg

arm

foot

tail

dinosaur
egg
tail
foot
head
nest
arm
leg

Spotting pairs of matching words helps children recognize and remember the shapes made by words.

5

Off to the museum

Cat plays "dinosaurs" all the way to the museum.
He stamps his feet and crashes about.
He swishes his tail and shows his teeth.
He hides in some bushes in the park, and shakes the branches to make Mouse jump.
   At last they reach the museum.
   "You can stop pretending to be a dinosaur now," says Mouse.
"There are plenty of them inside."

I spy in the museum

On their way to find the dinosaurs, Cat and Mouse play "I spy". First, Cat chooses something he can see and tells Mouse the sound of the first letter.

"I spy with my little eye something beginning with 'duh'," he says. Mouse guesses drum and he is right. Then it is his turn to choose something.

You can play "I spy" like Cat and Mouse. Look at all the things in the museum before you start.

dinosaur

This game will help your child gain practice with letter sounds. Point out or write down the letters as you choose them to help your child associate the sound with the correct symbol.

Mouse has a dinosaur ride

dinosaur

dinosaur

dinosaur

dinosaur

These pictures tell the story of Mouse's adventures with a dinosaur.

Can you tell the story out loud?

The purpose of this picture story is to encourage children to focus on what is happening in each picture and to translate this into words which build into a story.

What do you think the museum keeper would have said if he had seen
Mouse on the dinosaur?

This skill will be useful when your child comes to stories with words. Clues from the pictures
give children the confidence to try the words in the story.

11

The museum shop

Read this story with your child, pausing when you come to a picture. Let your child say the word for the picture and then carry on reading. Follow the lines with your finger as you read.

"Can I have my please?"

asks . He wants to

spend it in the museum

 opens his

and gives him some.

"Don't spend it all on  ,"

says  .

 buys a dinosaur

buys a dinosaur

buys a nice thick

dinosaur , and a

cuddly dinosaur toy for

Last of all, he buys a big

of dinosaur chocolates.

 wants to buy a dinosaur  .  sits on a  while  decides which one to have.  is feeling hungry and opens the  of dinosaur chocolates. They are delicious.

After a while,  starts feeling sorry for himself.

"What's the matter?" asks  .

"I don't feel well," groans  .

"I'm not at all surprised," says  . "You've just eaten a giant size  of dinosaurs."

Build a dinosaur

When Cat feels better, the museum keeper gives Cat and Mouse a game to play. Can you help by playing it with them?

head

arm

arm

head

leg

foot

tail

foot

tail

foot

dinosaur

How to play

To play this game you will need 10 small paper squares, a different counter for each player (you can use buttons or coins), and a dice. Each player chooses a dinosaur to build.
Start off by placing both counters on the arrow space. Players take turns throwing the dice and moving around the number of spaces shown. If you land

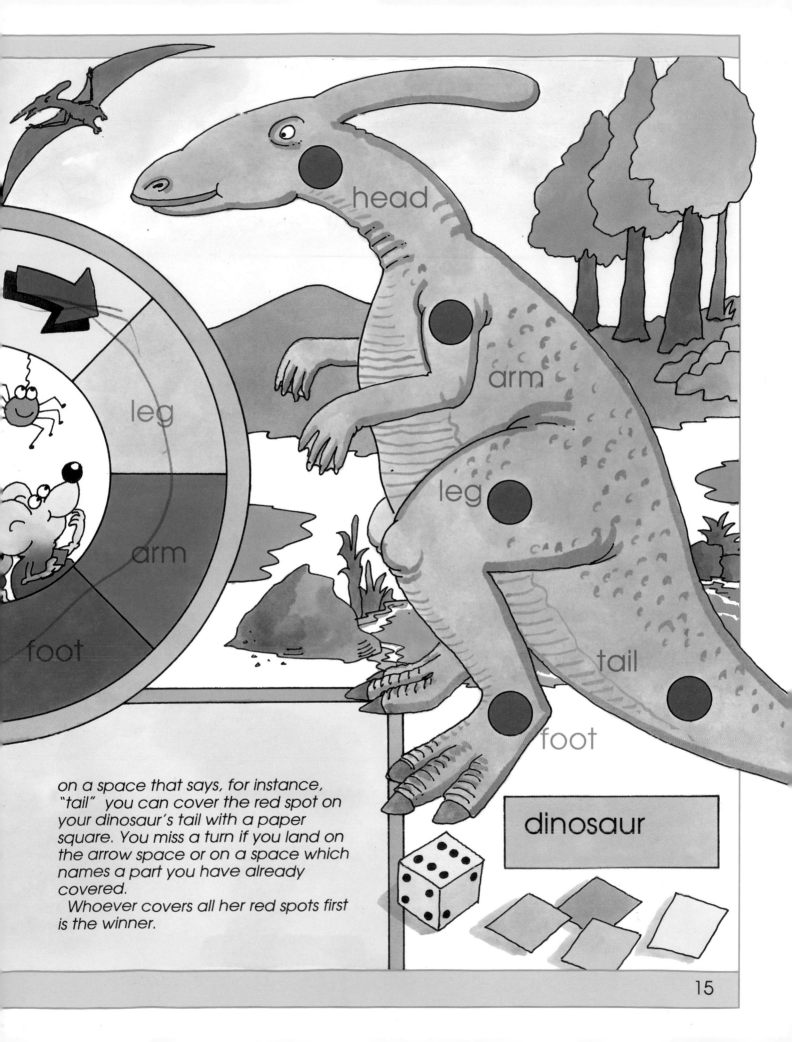

leg

arm

foot

head

arm

leg

tail

foot

dinosaur

on a space that says, for instance, "tail" you can cover the red spot on your dinosaur's tail with a paper square. You miss a turn if you land on the arrow space or on a space which names a part you have already covered.

Whoever covers all her red spots first is the winner.

Cat meets a dinosaur

Read this story with your child, following the lines with your finger. When you get to the words in blue type, stop and help your child to try reading them.

In the afternoon, Cat falls asleep in a warm, dark corner of the museum. What is he dreaming about?

   He dreams he is exploring the land of the dinosaurs, long long ago. He wears a safari hat and jungle boots, and stands on the top of a tall mountain. He can't see any dinosaurs.

   "I am Cat," he shouts. "I am brave and I'm not afraid of dinosaurs."

   All at once he hears a terrible noise, "Roaaar Roaaar Roaaaaaar," from behind the trees. A dinosaur is coming. Is Cat brave now?

No
Cat is scared.

He quickly hides behind a rock.
Thud - Thud - Thump!
The ground is shaking under his paws. Is Cat brave now?

No
Cat is scared.

Roaaar.... Roaaar.... Roaaar....

Your child will soon begin to recognize the repeating words and will have a sense of achievement from helping you read the story.

He curls up in a ball beneath a bush.
Creak - Crackle - Crash!
The trees and bushes bend and break, and
Cat can hear the snapping teeth. Is Cat
brave now?

No
Cat is scared.
He dives into a cave, where he shivers
and shakes until the dinosaur has gone.

When all is quiet, Cat comes out.
   "I wasn't afraid of dinosaurs," he
whimpers, "until I met one."

Dinosaur eggs

big

In Cat's dream, he and Mouse have found some dinosaur eggs that have fallen out of their nests. Suddenly, they hear the mother dinosaur coming and they hurry to put the eggs back. Cat collects all the eggs for the big nest and Mouse collects for the small nest. Play this game to help them put the eggs back in the right nests.

small

How to play

Cut out nine "eggs" from paper and place them in a pile between you. Make eight small cards. On three write "big", on another three write "small" and on the two left over draw a broken egg. Put all the cards in a bag . Play this game with the nests on the page.

One of you is Cat and one of you is Mouse. Take turns picking a card from the bag. Cat can put an egg from the pile in his nest if the card says "big", and Mouse can do the same if his card says "small". If, for instance, Mouse pulls out a "big" card he misses a turn. Also miss a turn if you pull out a "broken egg" card. Put the cards back after each turn.

When all the eggs are in the nests, count them to find out who has managed to put back the most.

small
small
big
big
small
big

The big egg

The words on this page are for you to read to your child. The words on the opposite page are for your child. Start by reading the pararaph below. Then encourage your child to try the words under the picture opposite. Take turns to complete the story.

Cat has been busy putting all the dinosaur eggs back in the nest. Just when he thinks they are all safely back inside the nest he sees one more egg lying all alone among the leaves.

"Not another one," says Cat. "My back hurts." He is just about to pick it up when a strange thing happens. The egg begins to wibble wobble all by itself.

"Eggs are not meant to wibble wobble like that," says Cat. "Something must be happening." He quickly calls Mouse to come and look.

Now the egg is not only wibble wobbling, but crick cracking as well.

"It will be a dear little baby dinosaur," says Mouse. "We can wrap it up and look after it and sing it to sleep."

CRACK! All at once, the eggshell breaks into tiny pieces and out hops a baby dinosaur. It has small, sharp teeth and it is very hungry. It begins to nip at Cat's tail,

"Go away, go away," shouts Cat.

"Get up, Cat," says a voice. It isn't a baby dinosaur, it is Mouse, pulling his tail to wake him up. "You are having a dream. They are closing the museum and we must go home."

Cat wakes up and rubs his eyes.

"Thank goodness it's you, Mouse," he says. "I thought you were a dinosaur."

In this shared reading activity, your child is given a simplified version of the adult text to read . Give lots of help and encouragement as some new words are introduced here.

Here is the egg.

Here is Cat. Here is the egg.

Here is Mouse. Here is Cat. Here is the egg.

Here is Mouse. Here is Cat. Here is the egg. Here is a dinosaur.

The dinosaur puzzle

1

Cat is here.

2

Here is a foot.

3

Here is a leg.

4

Here is a big tail.

This is a big step for your child. Read the story aloud first, if you like, then give lots of encouragement by suggesting your child looks carefully at the pictures. You can give first letter sounds as clues.

Here is a small arm.

Here is a head.

Here is a dinosaur.

Cat is scared.

Back at home

dinosaur

egg

small dinosaur

big dinosaur

The next day, Cat and Mouse have a lovely messy time painting the dinosaurs they had seen. They pin their pictures on the wall.

"They will frighten all our visitors," laughs Mouse.

Cat looks out of the window.

"It's stopped raining," he says. "Come on, Mouse. Let's go out to play." They quickly put away the paints and off they go.